RORY the Dinosaur
Needs a Christmas Tree

Liz Climo

Little, Brown and Company

New York   Boston

guess
what?

It's Christmas Eve on Rory's island!

Everybody is getting into the holiday spirit,

especially Rory and his dad.

They've hung their stockings

and made Christmas cookies.

Everything looks perfect, except for one thing.

So Rory and Dad put on their winter gear

and go looking for a tree.

Rory finds a great tree!

But it's a little too big.

Dad finds one too,

but it isn't very sturdy.

This tree might be perfect!

Nope, never mind.

This one isn't quite festive enough.

There are plenty of trees on the island,

but none of them seem to make a good *Christmas* tree.

I'm not sure
we're going to
find a
christmas tree.

Rory is disappointed, but it's time
to go home and celebrate.

hey, let's
get the
cookies ready
for santa.

Rory knows Santa can't have cookies without milk.

Suddenly, Rory hears something outside....

His friends are caroling at the window!

Rory and Dad invite them in for cocoa and
a Christmas story.

He has such a good time, he forgets why
he was ever feeling sad.

After his friends go home, Rory goes to put

Dad's gift under the tree

and remembers...

But then he thinks about how much fun he had
that day with Dad and all his friends...

...and eventually drifts off to sleep.

Soon, morning comes...

...and Rory wakes up to a twinkling on the windowpane.

MY VERY
OWN
CHRISTMAS
TREE!

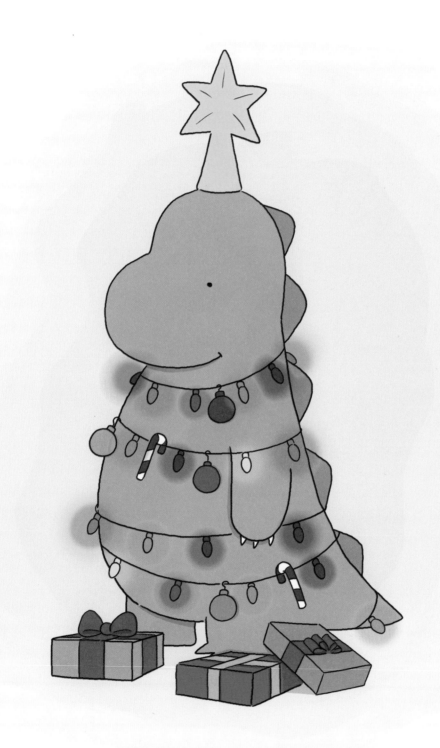

Rory's friends come over to exchange gifts.

check out
my christmas
tree! isn't it
so cool?!

But Rory knows Christmas isn't really about the tree.

It's about celebrating with family and friends

and being with the ones you love.

for my mom, who helped to make Christmas magic

About This Book

The illustrations for this book were done with digital magic. The text was set in CG Schneidler, and the display type was hand-lettered by the author. This book was edited by Mary-Kate Gaudet and designed by Jen Keenan and Gail Doobinin with art direction by Saho Fujii. The production was supervised by Erika Schwartz, and the production editor was Annie McDonnell.